ABC, WHAT DO YOU SEE?
ROLLING ALONG ROUTE 66

Written by Annette LaFortune Murray

Illustrated by Joyce Harbin Cole

atmosphere press

Anna Lee,
Happy Trails!
Annette LaFortune Murray

Published by Atmosphere Press

Library of Congress Control Number: 2022903414

atmospherepress.com

For my students who shared
the magic of reading with me.
—Annette

For my grandchildren:
Reid, Brett, Lorelai, Daisy, and Zoe.
—Joyce

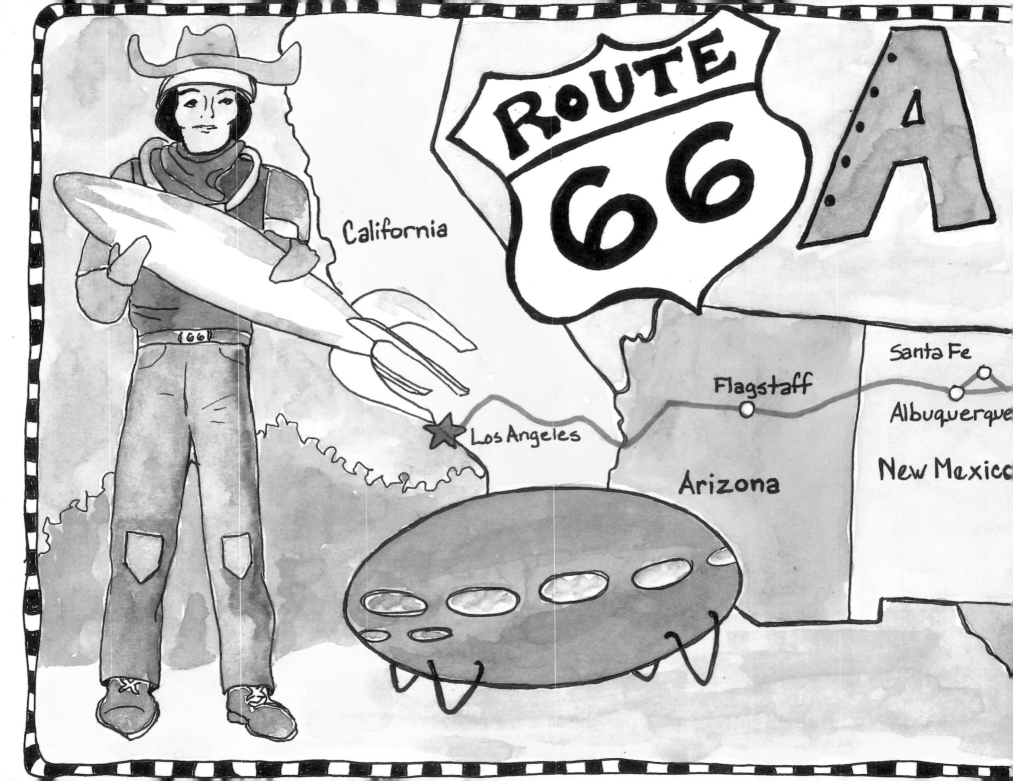

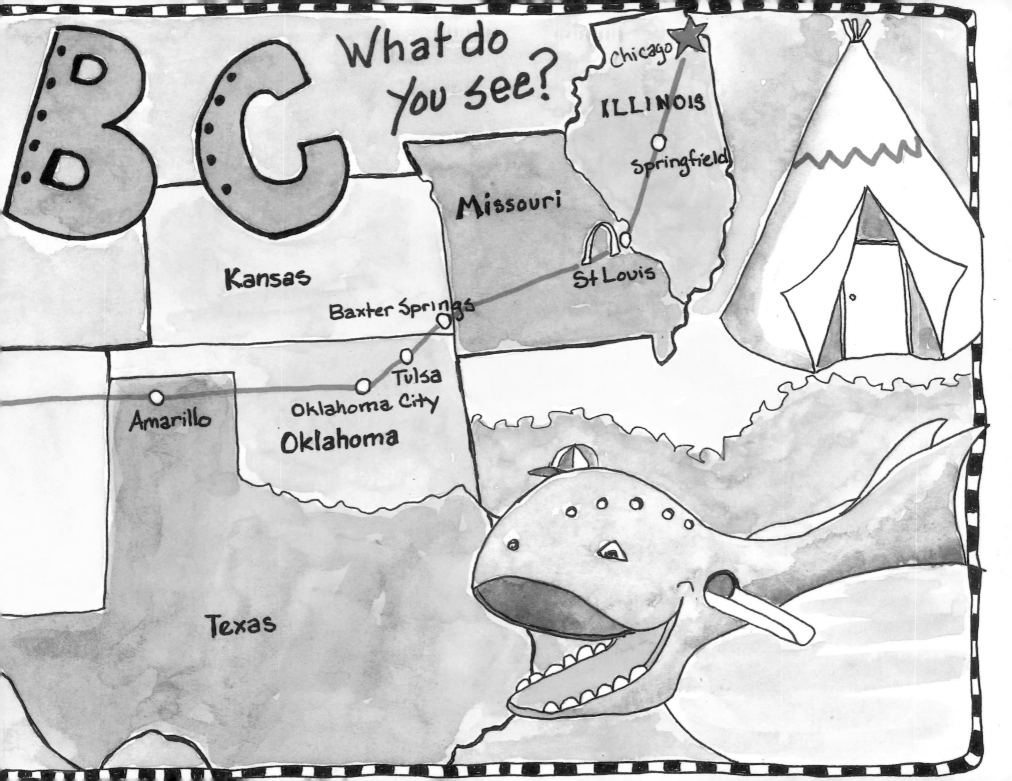

A is for America's Mother Road. Arched bridges. Amarillo and Albuquerque. Art on buildings. Art in Arizona canyons.

B is for Boots, Burgers, Buses, and the Buck Atom's Cosmic Curios cowboy.
Blue Swallow Motel with a neon Billboard. Bicyclists pedaling past Buffalo.

C is for Cyrus Avery, Father of Route 66.
Coffee in Cafes. Cameras Clicking in California.
Chain of Rocks Bridge.

D is for Drive-ins, Diners, and train Depots. Divernon. Daggett.
Deserts with cacti. Desserts with Dollops of whipped cream.
Dodger Stadium and Ted Drewes Frozen Custard.

6

E is for Eagles with Excellent Eyesight Entertaining bird watchers.
Eisler Brothers Store. El Rancho Hotel. Elwood. El Reno.

ELWOOD 5 mi.

7

F is for Filling stations Fixing Flat tires. A Ferris wheel twirling.
Flying squirrels above ground. Fossils Found underground.

SANTA MONICA

★ YACHT HARBOR ★
SPORT FISHING ★ BOATING
cafes

SANTA MONICA

66

End of the Trail

G is for the Gemini
Giant, Gift shops,
and Gila monsters.
Gateway Arch
Greeting sightseers
in St. Louis.
Gorgeous scenery
from Galena to Glendora.

H is for a Highway with History and Heritage, Half-way there at Adrian.
Harley motorcycles Humming along 2,448 miles.

I is for Inspirational architecture in Illinois.

Itty-bitty hummingbirds, Iconic art Installations, and Incredible Ice cream at Kix on 66.

J is for Joshua trees and Javelinas out West.
Jam in Jars and turquoise Jewelry at Jack Rabbit Trading Post.
Jesse James Wax Museum. Joliet. Jericho.

K is for the Kaleidoscope of sunrise colors in Kansas.
Knapsacks. Kayaks. Kan-O-Tex Service Station.

L is for License plates and
Landmarks in every state.

ROUTE 66

NEW MEXICO
US 66

New Mexico USA
Land of Enchantment

ROCK SHOP

Lou Mitchells

Lovely landscapes in La Verne, Lebanon, and Litchfield.
Luscious donut holes and Large omelettes at Lou Mitchell's.

M is for the Mississippi River and Meramec River Meeting in Missouri.
Memories Made visiting Monuments, Museums, and Muffler Men.
Musicians Making catchy Music on Route 66.

Joliet Area Historical Museum

JOLIET, IL
US
66

N is for National Parks. Neon signs illuminating the Night sky. Chefs in New Mexico creating Native dishes.

WESTWARD HO! MOTEL VACANCY

NATIONAL PARK SERVICE

PETRIFIED FOREST NATIONAL PARK

O is for the Cyrus Avery
Observation Tower at Lake
Overholser in Oklahoma.
Oil derricks, Overlooks, and an
O-shaped barn in Arcadia.

TULSA 66

17

P is for Postcards and Paintings
of historic Route 66.
People stamping Passports in Pontiac.
Pintail ducks, the Pink Elephant, and
Pops 66 Soda Ranch.

free Route 66 Pin

Nostalgic Relics from
The Mother Road, Photos, Iconic
Rt 66 Mural, the Bob Waldmire
VW and Road Yacht too!

18

Q is for Quirky attractions and Quarries with Quartz for rockhounds.
Queso and Quesadillas served in Quaint cantinas.

R is for Rattlesnakes, Roadrunners, and Robots. Roads marked with double sixes from Chicago to Los Angeles, Reaching over Rivers, across Ranches, and beside Railroad tracks.

20

S is for Sprague's Super Service Station and Scenic overlooks.

Suitcases and Sunglasses. Snakes under boulders and Soft-Shelled turtles creeping across highways.

T is for Tourists driving through Tulsa,
Tucumcari, and Topock. Travelers
Taking a break at TowerStation & U-Drop Inn Café.

U is for Uninterrupted highway from Chicago to Santa Monica.
Unexplained UFOs in Unexpected places.
Uphill climbs Underneath the scorching sun.

23

V is for Vacancy signs at motor courts where Vehicles and
Vans park for the night.
Vendors in Vintage shops selling Various souvenirs.

W is for Wildlife habitats and the Blue Whale of Catoosa.
Whimsical Wigwams Waiting for Weary travelers to sleep over.
Bob Waldmire's Wacky bus.

X is for cedar waXwings, creating Xs across the sky.

XC mountain bikes racing through canyons, along bluffs, and down hills.

Y is for Yarrow bushes dressed in Yellow flowers.
An unusually long Yearly Yard sale
stretching for 100 miles.
Cowboys Yelling, "Yippy-Ay-O!"
and "Yeehaw!"

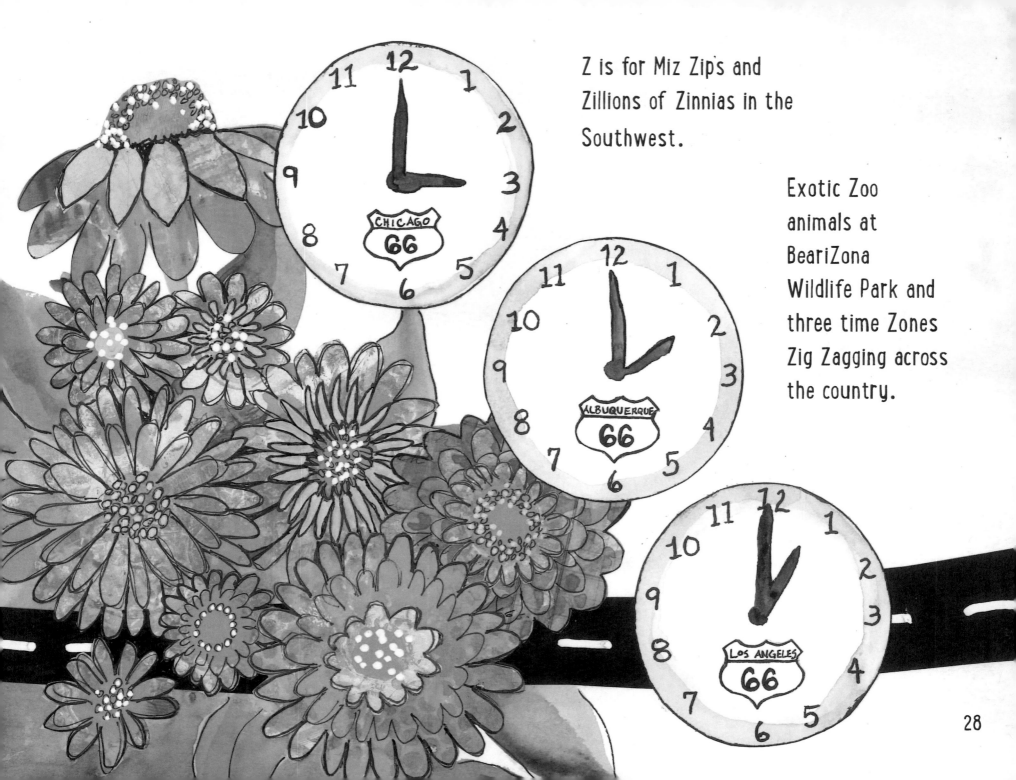

Z is for Miz Zip's and Zillions of Zinnias in the Southwest.

Exotic Zoo animals at BeariZona Wildlife Park and three time Zones Zig Zagging across the country.

Note from the Author

Welcome to Route 66! This book is the story of America's historic highway through the West. It is filled with people, places, wildlife, nature, architecture, and landmarks. When you travel on Route 66, you can soak up stories told by travelers, writers, musicians, business-owners, travel guides, and postcards.

When I was young, my family drove 60 miles from Tulsa to Grand Lake every weekend on part of Route 66. Now my husband and I visit different parts of Route 66 every year. I envision the highway as a chapter book of stories stretching half-way across America. Every stop is a page of interesting characters and plots from the past. It's like history comes alive! I hope you get to visit all or part of Route 66 someday. If you do, send me a postcard from some of your favorite stops. Mail your postcard to the address here.

Write to the author

Annette L. Murray
5103 S. SheridanRd.
Box #651
Tulsa, OK 74145

Route 66 Attractions You Can Find in this Book

ARIZONA

Jack Rabbit Trading Post	Joseph City, AZ
Miz Zip's	Flagstaff, AZ
Twin Arrows Trading Post	Flagstaff, AZ
Wigwam Hotel	Holbrook, AZ
Bearizona Wildlife Park	Williams, AZ

CALIFORNIA

Dodger Stadium	Los Angeles, CA
Joshua Tree National Park	Palm Springs, CA
Pacific Park Ferris Wheel	Santa Monica, CA

ILLINOIS

Bob Waldmire Bus	Pontiac, IL
Chain of Rocks Bridge	Madison, IL
Gemini Giant	Wilmington, IL
Lou Mitchell's Café	Chicago, IL
Pink Elephant Mall	Livingston, IL
Sprague's Super Station	Normal, IL

KANSAS

Kan-O-Tex Service Station	Galena, KS
Eisler Brothers Store	Riverton, KS

How Many Have You Visited?

MISSOURI

Chain of Rocks Bridge	St. Louis, MO
Gateway Arch Wax Museum	St. Louis, MO
Jesse James Wax Museum	Stanton, MO
Ted Drews Frozen Custard	St. Louis, MO

NEW MEXICO

Blue Swallow Motel	Tucumcari, NM
El Rancho Motel	Gallup, NM
Kix on 66	Tucumcari, NM

OKLAHOMA

Blue Whale	Catoosa, OK
Buck Atoms Cosmic Curios	Tulsa, OK
Observation Tower	Okla. City, OK
Historic Round Barn	Arcadia, OK
Pops 66 Soda Ranch	Arcadia, OK

TEXAS

Cadillac Ranch	Amarillo, TX
Tower Station & U-Drop Inn Café	Shamrock, TX

About the Author

Annette LaFortune Murray loves to travel. She started going on car trips with her family when she was five and continues to travel to new places and meet new people. As an elementary school teacher and librarian, Annette took her students on trips through the thousands of books she read to them. This is her first nonfiction picture book. Annette lives in Tulsa, Oklahoma near Route 66 with her husband, Kevin, and her West Highland Terrier, Sugar.

About the Illustrator

Joyce Harbin Cole has been drawing on things since she was able to hold a crayon, and she hasn't stopped yet. Running her Route 66 souvenir shop keeps Joyce inspired as she greets travelers from all 50 states and around the world. On her own adventures, Joyce keeps travel journals filled with drawings like the ones you see in this book. She lives with her Standard Poodle, Greta, just a few blocks from Route 66 in Pontiac, Illinois.

About Atmosphere Press

Atmosphere Press is an independent, full-service publisher for excellent books in all genres and for all audiences. Learn more about what we do at atmospherepress.com.

We encourage you to check out some of Atmosphere's latest releases, which are available at Amazon.com and via order from your local bookstore:

You are the Moon, a picture book by Shana Rachel Diot

Onionhead, a picture book by Gary Ziskovsky

Odo and the Stranger, a picture book by Mark Johnson

Jack and the Lean Stalk, a picture book by Raven Howell

Brave Little Donkey, a picture book by Rachel L. Pieper

Buried Treasure: A Cool Kids Adventure, a picture book by Anne Krebbs

Young Yogi and the Mind Monsters, an illustrated retelling of Patanjali by Sonja Radvila

The Magpie and The Turtle, a picture book by Timothy Yeahquo

The Alligator Wrestler: A Girls Can Do Anything Book, children's fiction by Carmen Petro

My WILD First Day of School, a picture book by Dennis Mathew

The Sky Belongs to the Dreamers, a picture book by J.P. Hostetler

I Will Love You Forever and Always, a picture book by Sarah Thomas Mariano

Shooting Stars: A Girls Can Do Anything Book, children's fiction by Carmen Petro

Oscar the Loveable Seagull, a picture book by Mark Johnson

Carpenters and Catapults: A Girls Can Do Anything Book, children's fiction by Carmen Petro

Gone Fishing: A Girls Can Do Anything Book, children's fiction by Carmen Petro

CPSIA information can be obtained
at www.ICGtesting.com
Printed in the USA
BVRC100919270222
629982BV00001BA/2